Professor Curiosity
vs.
Ermentrude Glock

By
Dave Magill

Contents

What cat?

'You need to be more careful, Noah,' said Mrs Fisher looking at her soaking wet son, 'Curiosity killed the cat you know.'

'What cat, Mum?' Noah replied with a confused look on his face, 'was it your cat? Is it buried in the garden?'

'Very funny, Noah,' his mum said ruffling his wet hair. Noah didn't get the joke. He'd have to ask Dad about the dead cat later. He also didn't know what that had to do with what had just happened.

Noah was one of those children that was fascinated by everything. He wanted to know what everything meant and how everything worked. He wanted to know where everything came from and how everything was made. He was very curious, just like the dead cat. His dad called him Professor Curiosity but it was just a nickname: Noah had never been to university.

That afternoon he had been playing in the garden when he decided to investigate the big, plastic tank at the bottom of one of the drain pipes at the side of the garage. He'd never seen anyone touch it before but it had always been there since the Fishers moved into the house. The bottom

5

of the green tank was hidden behind some old bricks that dad kept saying he was going to use to build something called a raised bed. Noah didn't understand who would sleep in a bed outside, and anyway, Dad hadn't moved those bricks in 2 years, even though Mum kept asking him to.

'You're a man of many great ideas and very little action,' she would say.

'You're so right, Love,' Dad would say, and then kiss her. Noah never liked it when they kissed in front of him. It looked disgusting.

Noah was sure that there must be some important use for that tank and was determined that he'd find out what was in it before dinner time. It was Friday. That meant dinner was his favourite food. He would celebrate his discovery with some tasty slices of cheese and tomato pizza.

Noah got the tools he needed, which were:
A plastic stick that used to be a tiny golf club but his little brother, Gideon, had broken it.
His little metal torch.
His plastic hard hat.
Some string he had found in the garage.

He would take some of the bricks and build a small staircase, and then climb up to investigate. Once he was at the top of his stairs he would decide what to do next.

Noah built his staircase, but it was a little wobbly. He climbed carefully and was soon at the top where he discovered a round lid with a lot of green moss on top of it. He took his plastic stick and scraped the moss away. This revealed a small groove and a handle. He pushed the stick into the groove and pushed down as hard he could. The lid began to move and then with a loud pop it opened.

It was dark inside the tank but thankfully Noah had his trusty torch. He turned it on and leaned over the tank, his waist resting on the edge of the opening. At that moment his wobbly staircase became even more wobbly and fell into a heap of bricks. Noah leaned forward some more so that he didn't fall to the ground but what happened next surprised even Professor Curiosity. He fell back and the tank fell with him. Just as he hit the soft grass behind the bricks a tidal wave of brown water came rushing out of the tank and almost washed Noah into the hedge.

'It's a water tank!' he shouted through the rushing water. 'It collects rainwater! I knew I could work it out!'

Noah was so excited to have discovered something new, that he seemed not to notice that he was soaking wet and filthy. That is when his mum came rushing into the garden with a shout.

'What are you doing? Look what you've done! What a mess, Noah.'

Things like this happened to Noah a lot. He thought of them as little adventures, but mum didn't seem to agree. Every time he was either soaking wet, covered in paint or glue or dust, she looked at him in that same way, and every single time she talked about that dead cat.

Some of his more recent investigations were;
- 1. Digging along the root of a tree that ran for 2 metres underground until he found the end. Result: he was so covered in mud that he had to be hosed down in the

garden before being allowed back into the house. The water was freezing.

- 2. How long does a tyre take to deflate? Result: one flat car tyre. One angry dad. One very late arrival at school.
- 3. How long does spray paint take to dry? Result: One ruined trainer. One ruined t-shirt. Two angry parents and a bright red thumb for two weeks.

Mum and Dad weren't often very pleased with his experiments, but his little orange notebook was filled with information about all sorts of things. For example; spray paint takes longer to dry on a piece of wood than on a trainer. A tree root can be more than 2m long.

Rainwater smells terrible if it's been a green plastic tank for a long time.

Noah loved investigating things. It got him in trouble sometimes, but mostly it gave him amazing, little adventures and discoveries. Sometimes, it also helped Noah to save the day.

Oak Heath Primary

Noah was in year 3 at Oak Heath Primary School but everyone knew it as Oaky's. If you're trying to work out how old he was, he was 7. Oaky's was on the north side of town, up on the hill. At lunchtime, Noah used to try and spot all the places he knew in the town below and would tick them off in his little book when he spotted them.

On the other side of town, the south side was Edward Bunkington Infant and Junior School but everyone knew it as Bunks. Oaky's and Bunks were arch-rivals; that means that they were always in competition with one another. It wasn't only the children who were competitive, it was their parents and even the teachers too. There was a rumour that a mum from Oaky's had once poured a whole, 2-litre bottle of milk over a Bunks mum's head in the supermarket because the other mum said that Bunks was better. Noah thought it was probably Stacey Priest's mum because she had a cross face and always seemed very angry.

There was nothing more important in the rivalry between Oaky's and Bunks than the annual Primary School football Championship. Every year, the two schools would battle it out on the football pitch to see who, for that year at least, were the true champions. These matches would have to have the police present because one year some parents got so angry that their child's school didn't win, that they chased the referee around until he had to climb up a lamppost for safety.

For the last three years, Oaky's has won the championship. In fact, they didn't just win it, they won it without losing a match or even letting in a goal. Noah's mum told him that the 2017-2019 Oaky's football team were the best team the school had ever had, and that she thought they could all turn professional one day.

There had been four superstar players in the school team for the past few years;

Alison 'The Ostrich' Gbeho
Pace:99
Shooting:78
Passing:90
Dribbling:89
Defence:40
Ability to bury her head in the
sand:0

Lennon 'Same Name' Lennon
Pace:60
Shooting:99
Passing:94
Dribbling:93
Defence:33
Ability to confuse referee:100

Daniel 'The Wall' Green
Diving: 95
Handling: 98
Kicking: 95

Speed: 80
Positioning: 91
Ability to hold up a roof: 0

These three legends of the game of football had left Oaky's the previous summer and had moved onto secondary school. This one star player behind - Esme Fisher, Noah's cousin.

If you think Alison, Lennon and Daniel were good players, Esme was even better. Esme was about to turn 11 but she had been playing in the school team since she was 7. She was fast and she was strong and she could play in any position. The previous year, in match 5 of the championship, Daniel had to miss the game because he had tonsillitis. Esme played in goal and didn't let a single shot anywhere near the net. Of all the superstars, Esme was the superest, which isn't even a real word - that's how super she was at football.

This year, Bunks thought they had their best chance in years of winning the championship. Oaky's only had one of their best ever players still at the school, and nobody knew anything about the children who had replaced them in the squad. They were all so new to the team that they didn't even have nicknames yet. Actually, that's not true, Daniel's little sister, Danielle was called 'The Little Wall' but that didn't really count.

Noah didn't play football. He was much more interested in the scoreboard, timekeeping and statistics. After every game Noah was the person who could tell you all the important things that happened in the game. He kept notes of things like;

- How many shots each team had.
- How many corners each team had.
- How many times a mum in the crowd told a dad off for using a word that he shouldn't.
- How many times the referee couldn't keep up with the game because they were an out of shape teacher who

didn't even want to be a
referee.
- How many goals were scored
and by whom.
- How many times Jason
Graham, the best player for
Bunks, stopped to make sure
his hair was looking just right.

Noah saw the important little
moments in the game better than
anyone else. He knew all the things
that added up to a win or defeat.
He didn't like playing football but he
liked understanding it. Maybe one
day he would be a commentator.

We should stop and talk about
Jason Graham. Jason was the star
of the Bunks team. He played as
their striker and was the only player
to score against Oaky's last

season. He was tall, fast and strong and he had amazing hair. He always had the best football boots available and there were rumours that he had a personal football coach who used to play for England, but nobody had ever worked out who it was. Jason was a great footballer and he knew it.

The Graham family lived on the same street as Esme and her parents, Aunt Susie and Auntie Sue - Middleton Lane. Mr and Mrs Graham owned Graham's Bubbles, a chain of shops that sold deodorant, soap and shower gel at discount prices. They also owned Graham the Chemist in the Main Street. It had been there for years. Mr Graham's father had set it up in the 1950s. It's where mum bought her vitamins because, as she said, 'you can trust the Graham name. They've been here for ages.' Noah wasn't so sure.

Esme and Jason had been best friends before they started primary school. They went to the same playgroups and learned how to kick a ball together in Esme's back garden when they were 3. Over the years, as they competed against each other in the yearly football championships, their friendship faded away. They were now competitors. They could be friends again once it was decided which team was best.

This was the last year they would play against each other. This was the big one. They would both start the same high school next year. They'd be allies again. They could forget about the rivalry after the summer. Until then, football was the most important thing. This year would settle it once and for all.

Neck and neck

The championship was played across 16 weeks. Every 4 weeks a game was played at one of the schools. Parents would take days off work to watch the game. It was the most exciting thing that happened every year. It was important to the whole town.

This year's championship did not start as Oaky's had planned. The first four-game results were as follows.

Game 1 - Location: Bunks.

Bunks   2-1   Oaky's

Graham 15, 92 (pen)
Fisher 22

Green (yellow) 92

The game reached the final minute
at 1-1 but The Little Wall tripped
Jason Graham in the box and he
scored the penalty.

Special stat: Number of times
Mums told Dads off for using words
that they shouldn't: 4.

Game 2 - Location: Oaky's
Oaky's   1-0   Bunks
Smith 1

A boring game after the 1st minute.
It was wet and muddy and horrible
to watch and even worse to play.

Special stat: Number of times referee considered ending the game early: 52

Game 3 - Location: Oaky's

Oaky's.	1-3	Bunks
Fisher 35 (pen)		
J. Graham 19,37		

M. Graham 88

Graham 2.0. Jason's little sister Miri played the last five minutes. She scored a header to add to Jason's two goals. Oaky's fans were not happy. One Graham was bad enough, two was much worse.

Special stat: Number of times Auntie Sue said, 'I wish she would pull her socks up. She looks so scruffy' : 10

Game 4 - Location: Bunks
Bunks   2-3   Oaky's
Graham 41.
Said 12, 34, 88
Li 66

A new superstar is born. 'Scoring' Samir Said scored all three goals. He wasn't even in the starting line up. Emily Anderson had to be subbed off in the 10th minute with a bruised head after walking into the post when waving at her dad in the crowd.

Special stat: Number of times kids said, 'is that really Samir? I can't believe it.': lost count.

Samir Said was in year 5 but he looked like he was in year 3. He was normally just the small and quiet guy who nobody knew much about, but on the pitch? He was amazing. He did things with the ball that surprised even Jason and Esme. By the end of the match, the crowd was singing his name. He was amazing.

It was neck and neck. It was far too close to predict who would win the deciding match. It could go either way and that made it even more exciting.

Back to school

The Monday after one of the big games was always a strange day, particularly if the team lost. It was as if the whole school became so focussed on the match the week before that even the headteacher, Mr Fowler, forgot about lessons. Getting back to work the next week was a shock for everyone.

The morning after game four passed by without much happening except for Mr Ford, the year 4 teacher, locking himself into his cupboard for 20 minutes. Some of the children in his class were sure they could hear him snoring in there, but when he finally got out of the cupboard, he told them they were imagining things.

By lunchtime, the big match of the week before felt like it had happened years ago. As Noah walked into the dining room with his lunchbox and drink he saw Esme.

'Hey, Noah. What's my favourite Auntie given you for lunch today?' she asked, giving him a little punch on the shoulder. Esme knew karate and the little punch hurt, but Noah tried to pretend it didn't.

'Same as usual. Chocolate spread tortilla, apricots, raisins, cheese, a packet of crisps and two fig rolls,' Noah said, considering giving

Esme a little punch back but instead just hovering his hand awkwardly in the air.

'What have my favourite aunts given you?' he asked Esme as they sat down.

'Oh, we are trying a new eating plan at home. Today I'm eating …' Esme started to say before being interrupted by someone banging on a table.

Every head in the room turned towards the noise to see Mr Fowler who was climbing onto a chair. Why do teachers do things that they tell children off for doing? Noah had been told off by Mr Fowler for standing on his chair a few weeks earlier. Noah had noticed that there was a spider on top of the bookshelf and he needed to get a closer look to know which species it was.

'Do you stand on a chair at home?' Mr Fowler had asked, as Noah had climbed down, and he seemed angry when Noah replied,

'All the time, Mr Fowler.' It was true. Noah didn't understand why that was the wrong answer.

It was even more confusing now that Mr Fowler was standing on a chair.

'Good afternoon, everyone. Some of you already know that last week was Mrs Murphy's last day as head of our school kitchen. After working at this school for almost 50 years she has retired and moved to Magaluf to follow her dreams of working as a DJ. Well, today I am delighted to introduce you all to our new head of the kitchen, Mrs Ermentrude Glock. Welcome, Mrs Glock with a round of applause, please.'

Everyone stood up to clap and Mrs Glock walked out of the kitchen and into the dining hall. Mrs Glock was very tall, though Noah noticed that she was wearing very posh high heel shoes. She had dark hair with a straight fringe that hid most of her face apart from very thick, black-rimmed glasses with brown coloured lenses. She had bright red lipstick and a round nose that looked like a painted ping pong ball.

'Hello, boys and girls. I'm Mrs Glock. It's nice to meet you. I'm looking forward to making delicious food in this kitchen. Some of my recipes are famous everywhere that people know about food,' said Mrs Glock. She spoke with a very croaky, but high pitched voice. It was a familiar voice to Noah but he had no idea why.

'I'm sure I've seen Mrs Glock before, Esme,' Noah said trying hard to remember.

'I don't think you'd forget someone like that, Noah. She's very, um, unique,' Esme whispered back. Aunt Susie had told Esme that it was rude to comment on people's hairstyles so she chose her words carefully.

After lunch, everyone was talking about how delicious the food had been. Mrs Glock has served pasta with vegetarian sausages all covered in her secret sauce that she called Glockognese.

Every day that week there was a new recipe;

Monday: Glockognese
Tuesday: Glock in the hole - Toad in the Hole but instead of sausages there was a cheeseburger in batter.
Wednesday: Chicken Glocka Masala - This was a normal tikka masala but the secret ingredient

seemed to be cheese and onion crisps.

Thursday: Glock dogs - A reverse hot dog. A very big sausage cut into a slice and a bread bun was put in the middle.

Friday: Glock and Cheese - This was like every mac and cheese anyone had seen before but for some reason, it was served in a small bucket.

Everyone loved the food. The new menu was the same every week and by the third week, everyone had their favourite Glock Meal with Chicken Glocka Marsala being the most popular of all. Esme and Noah watched from the packed-lunch table wishing their parents would let them get their food from

Mrs Glock's kitchen. Maybe one day their parents would let them.

A Sad Saturday for Samir Said

On the Monday before the final game of the season, Noah arrived at school to see Esme waiting for him at the door to his classroom. She had a strange look on her face. Noah wasn't sure what that look meant, but he guessed she was either angry or sad. As he saw her he realised a lot of people in school had that look on their faces.

'Hey, Esme. Good weekend?' Noah said smiling at his cousin.

'My weekend doesn't matter Noah. Haven't you heard what happened,' Esme replied? She was clearly worried about something.

'No,' Noah shrugged.

'Something weird had happened to Samir. He woke up on Saturday morning and told his mum he had a weird feeling in his head and by 11 am his head had become ten times the size it should be. It's too heavy for him to get out of bed. He can't get his pyjamas off without cutting them and he's refusing because they are his favourite set. The doctors have no idea what has happened because they've never seen anything like it.'

Noah was shocked. Noah loved reading biology books that he found in the library but he'd never heard of anything like this.

'I hope he's okay,' he said, 'he must be scared.'

'I know. Me too. We need him for the game this week. He's one of our best players,' Esme was very worried, 'We need him, Noah,' she said before heading off to her classroom.

All morning, all Noah could think about was poor Samir. What a horrible thing. By lunchtime, Samir was old news as more weird things had happened at the school.

Half-way through guided reading class, Amy Church, who was sat next to Noah began to fidget and move about in her chair. Amy played in defence for the team. She was really tall and really strong. Everyone in Noah's class was scared of Amy because she was so big compared to them but she was a gentle person who didn't get angry with anyone, except when she played football.

'I - I - I feel weird,' she said tapping Noah's arm.

Noah turned around and couldn't believe what he saw next. Amy began to shrink. Noah watched as she went from being well over 150 cm tall to no more than 30 cm tall. Her tiny head was just visible over the desk and she was screaming in a high pitched voice.

Before any of the children could react, Mrs Jones, Noah's teacher had bundled the tiny Amy up in her jumper and was running down the hall to the head teacher's office. The whole of Noah's class was gathered around the door staring after Mrs Jones as she ran off with Amy. Nobody said a word.

At that moment Mr Nenge, Esme's teacher, burst out of his classroom carrying James Andrews and Chloe Li, one under each arm. Both children were, just like Amy had been, only about 30 cm tall and were wrapped in their school coats.

Esme appeared at the door and looked across the hallway at Noah.

'What is going on?' She mouthed to him with shock on her face.

Noah didn't know what to say but whatever it was that was going on, it was like nothing anyone had seen before.

Weirder and weirder

Over the next two days, things got even weirder. By Wednesday, 7 people had been affected in strange ways by whatever was happening at the school. One person had suddenly turned to jelly, they looked the same but were a lot more wobbly, and couldn't do much apart from lie as still as they could (which wasn't very still at all). Another, Maya Nowak, had inflated like a balloon, and they had no way of getting her out of room 11, they'd had to move a fold-up bed in there for her to sleep in.

The final person to be affected,
The Little Wall, Danielle Green,
had woken up and her left hand
was on her right arm and her right
hand was on her left arm. The
same had happened with her feet.
This might not seem like a big deal
but it was. She couldn't do even
the simplest things because her
brain kept sending signals to the
wrong place.

The police were called in and every
doctor and expert on weird
diseases visited the school but
nobody had any idea what was
going on. Nobody had ever seen
anything like this before.

On Wednesday lunchtime, Esme
and Noah were sitting eating their
chocolate tortilla and experimental

packed lunches when Esme
suddenly realised something.

'Noah. What do you notice about
all the people who have had these
weird things happen to them?' She
asked.

Noah started to think of an answer
but before he'd even started
thinking Esme answered her own
question.

'That's right, Noah. They are all on
the football team. There are only
me and a few other players left and
it's the big game this Saturday. If
this doesn't stop the whole team
will be out of action. Even you
might have to play.' Esme seemed
very worried.

'It's either a very unlucky coincidence, Esme, or something very fishy is going on,' Noah said realising that deep down he was very suspicious about the whole thing. 'We should keep our eyes open for any clues of what might be going on,' he said, looking at Esme, 'do you want to go and play wallball to take our minds off it?' he asked, hoping he could cheer his cousin up.

'Yeah. Let's do that,' she replied, putting on her coat.

Wallball was an Oaky's tradition. The story goes, that it had always been played at the school. Wallball was played with a tennis ball and a wall. Each player took turns to throw the ball onto the ground to bounce it up against the wall. The other person had to catch the ball before it bounced on the ground three times after hitting the wall. It got very competitive and some of the older children played it at lightning speed. It almost got banned one year after two children lost their front teeth from running into the wall when trying to catch the ball - ouch!

Noah wasn't great at wall ball but he enjoyed thinking up the best angles to throw the ball at to make other people miss their catches. His problem was that he spent too much time thinking about angles and not enough time watching the ball. Today was no different. Almost every time Esme took a throw, Noah missed the catch. He spent most of the game running after the ball and reaching under benches or into bushes to retrieve it.

After about ten minutes of the game, Esme threw the hardest throw of all. It bounced high into the air and sailed over Noah's head, over the wall at the edge of the play area, and into the hedge on the other side of the wall. Noah ran after it and gently hopped over the wall. He peered into the bushes and then spotted the ball lying in the staff car park just on the other side of the hedge. Fortunately, there was a little hole in the hedge, just big enough for him to crawl through to grab the ball.

Noah got down on his hands and knees and crawled through old leaves, stones and dirt towards the ball. Just as he was about to emerge into the car park he heard the clip-clop of someone coming. He ducked back into the hedge. He didn't know if he'd get into trouble for being in the staff car park but he didn't want to find out either, so he decided to wait where he was.

As the clippy-cloppy feet came closer, Noah realised it was Ermentrude Glock, the new head of the school kitchen. She walked over to her car, which was a very flashy, convertible, Italian sports car. She jumped in and Noah watched as the roof began to fold back and into a little compartment in the boot. Noah loved watching how machines worked so this was a real treat.

Just as the roof was about to completely disappear from the car, Noah saw something he'd never expected to see. Ermentrude Glock took her nose off. Noah couldn't believe his eyes. She just reached up and pulled her round nose off and revealed a smaller nose underneath, she then took off her glasses and eventually took off her hair, which it turns out was a wig. It was at that moment that Noah realised that Ermentrude Glock sounded familiar because she was familiar. She lived on Esme's street: Ermentrude Glock wasn't really Ermentrude Glock at all. Ermentrude Glock was actually Mrs Graham, Jason Graham's mum.

Jason Graham from Bunks. What was she doing at Oaky's in disguise and working in the kitchen? Noah needed to talk to Esme.

After School

That afternoon, Noah was going home to Esme's house because both of his parents had to work. Auntie Sue collected them in her 1970s camper van and drove them home.

On the way to Middleton Lane Esme told Auntie Sue everything and all the weird things that had happened that day. Auntie Sue didn't seem to hear what was being said because she was very busy concentrating on driving. Auntie Sue drove whilst leaning over the steering wheel until her nose was almost pressed against the glass.

She was a very nervous driver, unlike Aunt Susan who was way too relaxed, and always drove as if she was in a race.

Noah was so desperate to talk to Esme about what he had seen in the car park but didn't want anyone else to hear. When they eventually arrived on Middleton Lane, Noah waited until he and Esme were in the lounge alone before he said anything.

'Esme. I saw something,' he said.

'Was it one of my mum's weird plants? They're called succulents I think but they look like cacti to me,' Esme said trying to find the remote control for the TV.

'No, at school, when I lost the ball. I saw something then,' Noah whispered.

'Oh. What did you see?' Esme didn't seem interested.

'Well, I was halfway into the staff car park when I saw Mrs Glock appear and go to her car but then I saw her take off a wig, glasses and even her nose. She was in disguise,' Noah was almost running out of breath as he finally got to tell Esme what he'd seen.

'Did you get a good look at her?' Esme was now very interested.

'Yes and Ermentrude Glock is actually Mrs Graham, from this very street, in disguise,' Noah finally got out what he needed to say and he dramatically fell back in his seat.

'Jason's mum? That Mrs Graham?' Esme asked with a little bit of panic in her voice.

'Yes, Esme, that Mrs Graham, and if my suspicions are correct I think there will be a link between Mrs Graham and what's been happening to all of the football team at school. I don't know how, Esme, but I think Mrs Graham is sabotaging our team, and we need to find out how she's doing it.'

Noah had always wanted to be a detective or a spy. One Christmas he had received a spy kit with lots of gadgets and binoculars and everything anyone needs to investigate a situation like this. He carried most of that spy kit with him to school every day just in case. If you ever meet his mum or teachers, don't tell them that, they'd be angry - school is for learning, not spying.

'Let's go and investigate, Noah,' Esme said, 'we have to find out what is going on. We can tell my mum we are going to see if Jason is in. Hopefully, she'll be too distracted to listen.'

Esme was right. Her mum was too distracted to listen. She was cooking from a book and, like a lot of grown-ups, she found it very hard to do more than one thing at a time. Reading, cooking and listening were too much for her grown-up brain to handle.

'Yes, Essy. Sounds good,' she said as she tried to cut a piece of garlic up until it looked like the one in the photo in her recipe book, 'don't be late for dinner!'

'Yes, mum,' Esme said as she ran out the front door with Noah.

The Garage

A few moments later the two children were crouched down next to some boxes in the narrow alleyway beside the Graham family's garage. They could hear Mr and Mrs Graham in the garage talking.

'So how many players are left?' Mr Graham asked his wife.

'Four left and one of them is Esme. She takes her own lunch to school, so it's a lot harder to get her to take the potion. The others will be a lot easier. Nobody suspects a thing,' Mrs Graham said proudly.

'I knew she was up to something,' Noah said, writing notes down in his orange notebook.

'She's feeding potions to the football team. She wants to feed me a potion!' Esme was angry. 'She can't get away with this, Noah. We are going to get her back.'

'What's the plan, Esme?' Noah whispered to his cousin who didn't have a plan but wanted to look confident.

'We wait until they're gone and then you climb on my shoulders and look in the garage window to see what's going on. Maybe that will give us some ideas of what to do next,' she replied, secretly pleased that her on-the-spot plan seemed almost like it made sense.

After what seemed like hours, although it was only a few minutes, Esme and Noah heard Mr and Mrs Graham leave the garage. They looked both ways before Esme crouched down in front of the window.

'Okay, Noah, climb on my back and take a look,' she said, pointing towards her back as if Noah didn't know what she meant.

Noah stood up, took a deep breath, and then gently climbed onto his cousin's shoulders. He felt like he was going to fall off from the moment he was up there. He grabbed tightly to the ledge of the window and slowly peaked his eyes over the window frame. His mouth dropped open - he couldn't believe what he was seeing.

Back at Noah's house, their garage was filled with old bits of wood, garden toys and bikes. There were also boxes full of unknown things because Noah's parents had not opened them since they moved in. Those boxes were on Noah's list of things to investigate. He was just waiting for the right moment.

This garage was nothing like his parents' garage at all. The Graham's garage looked like a professional chemistry laboratory. The walls and countertops were pure glistening white. There were shelves of books and little bottles and jars of liquids and powders of all kinds. The bottles and jars had labels with letters and numbers on them that Noah recognised as the chemistry codes for molecules. His grandad had bought him a chemistry book when he was 6. On one wall of the garage was a large poster with those same letters and numbers. Noah recognised this as the Periodic Table of Elements from his chemistry book.

Right in the middle of the room, on top of the counter was the most complicated scientific experiment that Noah had ever seen. It was metres and metres of tubes and bulbs and flasks and droppers. At one end was something that looked like a candle but made of metal,

Noah thought it was called a burner. At the other end was a test tube that was slowly filling up with a bright purple liquid. On the table beside the experiment was a countdown clock that said, 35 minutes.

The final thing in the garage was a row of three small bottles with little droppers in them. The labels of the bottles said;

Head Swelling - 4 drops
Body inflating - 2 drops
Shrinking - 1 drop per metre.

'What's in there, Noah? I can't hold you much longer,' Esme suddenly hissed. She was clearly starting to struggle under Noah's 25 kg.

'I'll come back down and tell you. I have an idea,' Noah said as he climbed back off his cousin's shoulders and began to her all about what was inside the garage.

'If we can just find a way to get inside that garage and get some of those potions, we can plan how to use them ourselves,' Noah said, and just as he did the noise of the big garage door opening interrupted him.

Esme and Noah dropped down low and listened. They could hear someone round the front of the garage. Esme crept slowly to look.

'It's Jason,' she said, 'I'll distract him, you sneak inside.'

Esme waited a second before walking out into the driveway of the Graham's house at a moment when Jason was looking the other way. He'd never know what direction she'd appear from.

'Hi, Jason. Ready for the big game?' she asked her neighbour and footballing rival.

'Oh. I'm much more ready than ever. We are going to win this year, Esme,' Jason said in a voice that made Esme want to use all of her karate moves on him at once.

'Oh yeah, well, I wouldn't be too sure. You have such a weak team this year, starting with you,' Esme replied trying to get into an argument with Jason. It worked,

Jason was suddenly trying to prove how strong, fast and skilled he was to Esme who just stood listening.

Meanwhile, Noah crept behind Jason and into the open garage door. He had thought the laboratory looked cool from outside but inside it was even more impressive. Noah was mesmerised by all of the scientific instruments and chemicals. He suddenly remembered that he wasn't there to explore, he was there to grab a bottle and rush back out.

He realised just in time because just as he rounded the doorway and back into the alleyway, not only did the argument between Jason and Esme stop, but Mr

Graham opened the front door and walked into the driveway.

'Jason, stop arguing with the enemy and get in the car. We are going to have a barbecue and I forgot to buy burgers,' he said as he got into their car.

'Bye Esme. See you on the pitch,' Jason sneered as he closed the car door.

As Jason as his dad sped off down the street, the two cousins looked at each other with relief. They had managed to pull off step one of the plan. Now they had to work out what step two should be.

'Let's get back to my house and work out what to do next, Noah,'

Esme said. The two cousins
walked back up the street to make
a plan.

Target Practice

Noah stood at the window of Esme's room trying to think of what to do. It was one thing for a school cook to put potion into a pupil's meal, it was something else for a pupil to do the same. They just didn't have the chance to get close enough to the Graham's kitchen to do anything like that.

Just as Noah began to lose hope, he spotted Mrs Graham walking out of her back door and into her garden. She was carrying salad and plates to the outside table. She went back inside again but this time she returned with some glasses and bread.

'Esme. Do you still have that water pistol my mum bought you last year? You know, the big pump action one?' Noah asked, suddenly realising he had a plan after all.

'It's under the bed. What good will that be though?' Esme asked her cousin. Esme was frustrated and grumpy after she argued with Jason. He knew how to make her mad.

'Look. Mrs Graham is getting ready for their barbecue. She's put out salad, bread and plates. If I am guessing right, then she is going to go back inside and get drinks too. If we can use your water pistol and put some of one of these potions into it we might just be able to reach that drink with the potion,' Noah was excited. His plan might just work.

'You'd have to be a good shot to do it, Noah,' Esme wasn't so sure.

'Oh, Esme. Not me. You. You will do it easily,' Noah answers. He knew Esme was much better at these kinds of things.

The two children suddenly moved into action. Esme grabbed the water pistol and Noah carefully opened one of the bottles. The bottle was 500 ml which, if his calculations were right, would mean that Esme had three shots worth potion. If she missed with those then the plan would fail.

As Noah carefully poured the contents of the potion bottle into the water pistol he noticed for the first time that he had chosen the shrinking potion. If this worked, the Graham's would shrink to the size of a school ruler. That would make them very easy to handle.

Esme opened her window as wide as it would open and the two watched as, just as Noah had expected, Mrs Graham appeared with a large glass jug full of blackcurrant and apple squash. This was perfect. It was the ideal cover to hide a few drops of the purple potion in.

Noah and Esme watched and
waited for Mrs Graham to go back
inside. As she left the garden Esme
got into position, on one knee and
leaning her elbow on the
windowsill. She closed one eye
and her tongue slipped out of the
corner of her mouth. She always
did this when she concentrated, so
did Noah.

'Okay, Esme, good luck,' Noah
said. He was nervous. They didn't
have a lot of time and they only
had three chances to get this right.

Esme pulled the trigger and a small
jet of purple liquid shot into the air.
It was as if time slowed down as
they watched it move across the
neighbour's garden and towards
the Graham's table before hitting

the fence about 10 cm from the top.

'Ahh. Nooo.' Esme said angrily.

'Good first shot, Esme. You've got this,' Noah tried to encourage his cousin.

Esme took a deep breath and took her second shot. This time the red potion made it over the fence. The two cousins stood up slowly watching it loop towards the table.

'I think you've done it!' Noah said excitedly, 'ahhh noo. So close. Almost perfect, Esme,' he said as the potion splashed on the side of the jug and dropped through the holes in the metal table to the pebbles below.

'Right. Come on Esme. You can do this,' Esme said gently tapping her hands on her forehead.

She settled herself again and took her aim. She pulled the trigger and the final shot of potion shot into the air. Noah couldn't breathe as he watched. It passed over the fence. Esme stood up just in time to see the potion rise above the lip of the jug and splash into the juice with a plop.

'Yesssss!' they shouted, jumping up and down before quieting themselves again. They crouched down and peered over the window sill.

'Now we wait,' Noah said, realising he had to come up with what to do next.

A box of Grahams

Twenty minutes passed and the Grahams were out in the garden. Mr Graham was at the barbecue cooking sausages. Mr Graham didn't ever cook anything else. He only cooked barbecues. Noah's dad was the same. Dad's must really like barbecues.

Jason was kicking a ball at the back of the garden with his little sister and Mrs Graham was sat on a chair reading a magazine about gardening. Each of them was sipping a glass of the blackcurrant and apple juice with the shrinking potion in it.

Noah and Esme had no idea how long the potion would take to work but at least they knew it was being drunk by the Grahams. Noah was worried that they were only sipping their drinks. He was sure that they would need more than a sip to be affected by the potion.

Mr Graham served up his badly burnt hot dogs to his family and Noah and Esme instantly had a stroke of luck. All four Grahams bit into their hotdogs and instantly chugged down their whole glass of juice.

'Urgh. What are these, John?' Mrs Graham shouted, waving her hand in front of her open mouth, 'my mouth is on fire.'

Mr Graham lifted the sausage packet up and read the label.

'Gluten Free Dangerously Hot Chilli and Tabasco Pork Sausages,' he said looking very puzzled, 'I was sure I lifted them from the normal gluten-free pile.'

'You didn't read the package, did you? Again. How many times is that now? You can't just assume, John. I'm amazed that you can run a chemist safely.' Jason's mum was very angry and her face was almost purple, though that could have been the sausages or the anger.

'Muuum. Daaaad. I feel weird,' Jason interrupted.

Esme and Noah couldn't believe what happened next. They watched as not only Jason, but his little sister and his parents began to shrink. Within 30 seconds they were about 30 cm tall and looked even smaller sitting on their normal-sized garden chairs.

'Ha! Revenge!' Esme shouted punching the air. 'They deserve that.'

'What do we do now Esme? Our friends are still small and ballooned and big headed and jelly. Danielle's hands and feet are on the wrong sides. Revenge is one thing but we can't just leave them like that,' Noah was desperately trying to think of something to do next, 'we have to get the antidote. There must be an antidote to get them back to normal. An antidote is the potion that will reverse the other potions, Esme.'

'I know what an antidote is!' Esme said, rolling her eyes.

The two stared at each other trying to think of a plan before Noah stood up and loudly said,

'I need a box, Esme. We need to put them in a box and tell them that if we don't get the cure for our friends, that they will never get back to normal size again.'

'What if they don't give us it, Noah?' Esme was good at seeing all the ways a plan might not work out.

'We will cross that bridge when we come to it,' Noah replied.

'Will this do?' Esme said, holding up an old toy box that looked like a fire-engine.

'Perfect, let's go,' Noah replied, and was already halfway out of the room and heading to the Grahams' garden.

Catch

Once they had arrived in the Grahams' garden, Esme and Noah realised that catching a 30 cm tall human is much harder than you would think. They are very fast-moving and can get into nooks and crannies that a full-sized human can't. If you add into the mix that once Esme and Noah had arrived in the garden the Grahams' quickly worked out that they had been the ones who had put the shrinking potion in there drinks, then catching the four little Grahams became very difficult indeed.

Miri Graham was the easiest to catch. She ran behind a plant pot and hid under some leaves, but didn't realise her legs were still sticking out. Esme grabbed her by both her feet and gently lowered her into the box and put the lid on. You could here very squeaky shouts coming from the box but Noah and Esme ignored them.

Just at that moment, Noah spotted one of those fishing nets made of a net, a hoop and a long bamboo stick, lying beside the Graham's pond. He grabbed the net and very quickly managed to catch Mr Graham, who had been hiding behind the shed and had decided to make a run for it. As he crossed the garden Noah swooshed down the fishing net and lifted Mr

Graham into the air. Esme opened
the box and Noah dropped the little
man inside. Now to find the final
two Grahams.

The garden had gone very still and
quiet. Jason and his mum had
obviously chosen to hide. Esme
and Noah scanned the garden,
looking for little feet or a shadow
that might give away the location of
the final two runaways.

'I've got an idea,' Esme said
walking towards the Graham's
house. She lifted a long, rolled up
hose from the ground and turned
on the outside tap. The hose had
one of those ends on it that only
sprayed water when you pulled the
little lever. Esme waited a minute,
to let the pressure build up, and

started spraying every possible hiding place in the garden with a mist of cold water. To a normal-sized human that mist is quite a pleasant experience but if you were 30 cm tall it would be like being caught in a really bad rain storm.

Esme sprayed the hose over the bushes and behind the shed and across the firewood pile. As she moved down across a beautiful flowerbed the spray of water hit a big garden gnome with a long beard and little sign that said, 'No Place Like Gnome.' 'No Place Like Gnome' is the kind of joke that grownups start to find funny when they are about 35 years old. If you don't find it funny, don't worry, you will when you are older.

As the water soaked the gnome there was a sudden very high pitched squeal and both Jason and his mum ran out into the wet mud of the flower bed and were both instantly up to their knees in brown sticky mud. This made them much easier to catch. Noah ran over, grabbed the final two Grahams, one in each hand as if they were little dolls and put them into the box and pushed down the lid.

'Good work, Esme,' Noah said with a grin, 'that was quite fun. Now, let's take them into the garage and try and talk to them.'

Noah and Esme carried the box into the Graham's garage-laboratory and set it on the floor. They stared around them at the science equipment, chemicals and books that lined the walls. Both children loved science and would have loved to have a garage like this one day which they could use to carry out secret experiments.

Noah lifted a large plastic tub off one of the shelves. It looked like one of those tubs that grownups use to keep cereal in after a little brother or sister has destroyed the box. He unclipped the lid and looked at Esme.

'Okay. We are going to take out Mrs Graham and put her in this tub,' he said to his cousin, 'It is big enough to hold her in, has a lid to stop her escaping, but a big enough hole at the top to stop her running out of air to breathe.'

He set the tub onto the workbench next to the bubbling experiment that he had seen earlier. Without a moment of hesitation, Esme opened the box, reached her hand in and lifted out the little Mrs Graham. As she closed the box she could hear the quiet voices of the other Grahams shouting at her, but she ignored them. She plonked Mrs Graham into the plastic tub and Noah clipped the lid back on, making sure that there was enough air getting in.

Mrs Graham spent the next five minutes trying to climb up the sides of the tub, but each time she did she slid back down to the bottom. Eventually, she realised that she was wasting her time and sat down calmly with her back against the side of the tub. She looked like she was one of the animals in a very strange zoo, and Noah and Esme were staring at her in a way that made her feel exactly that way.

'Mrs Graham. Mrs Graham,' Noah said trying not to be too loud, 'look at me, up here.'

Mrs Graham slowly turned her face to look at Noah's face, which was almost as tall as she was. She was angry, her plan had gone wrong and now she was dealing with two giant children who knew exactly what she was up to.

'This is what is going to happen, Mrs Graham. If you ever want to be back to normal size again, you're

going to show us where the anti-
dotes for the potions you used on
our friends are. If you don't, we will
leave you as the tiny version of
yourself forever,' Noah said trying
to sound like he was in charge.
Noah tried to use the same kind of
voice his dad used when he was
trying to stop Gideon and Noah
from throwing water out of the bath.

Mrs Graham was shaking her head
and talking very quickly. She was
waving her arms around as she
spoke but neither of the children
could hear her from outside the
tub. Esme opened the lid a little
and said through the gap,

'You're going to have to say that
again, we can't hear you.'

She put her ear to the gap as Mrs Graham started to talk again before sitting back down in the tub.

'What did she say, Esme?' Noah asked expectantly.

'It's not good news, Noah. She hasn't made them yet,' Esme said, her eyes wide with disbelief.

Noah put his mouth to the open lid of the tub.

'You're going to have to show me how to make them then, Mrs Graham. It's the only way anybody is going to get back to normal.'

Mrs Graham stared up at the giant-to-her but normal to everyone else sized Noah before nodding and mouthing, 'okay.' She then did an impression of someone writing and pointed at her chest.

Noah looked around the room and found a little pink pad of sticky notes and one of those pencils that grownups have that is made of plastic and you push the end to make the lead come out. He pushed the end until about 1 cm of lead came out which he then broke off. He opened the lid and gently dropped the pad and the broken lead into the tub with Mrs Graham. She nodded back and grabbed the lead. Even though it was so tiny it still looked like a giant pencil in her little hands. She knelt on the sticky note pad and began to write.

'There is a book on the top shelf of the cabinet. The label says 'the after plan,' It has the instructions for how to make the antidote. It's the same antidote for all the potions.'

'Thank you, Mrs Graham,' Esme and Noah said at the same time before running across the garage to the cabinet. The top shelf was at least a metre higher than either of them could reach but Esme didn't hesitate to climb the shelves before throwing a small brown notebook to the floor below. Noah grabbed the book and flicked through the pages. Almost all of the pages were blank but then, halfway through the book, were 5 pages of writing and diagrams entitled, 'The Cure.'

He read it carefully and read it again.

We're going to need to wear those safety goggles, Esme,' Noah said pointing to two pairs of goggles on the countertop before grabbing a pair for himself and passing the other pair to his cousin. 'This is going to be fun but we have to get it exactly right, or who knows what could happen.'

Noah and Esme, Professors of Chemistry.

Noah and Esme hunched over the book and read the handwritten instructions three times. They needed to be sure that they got the experiment exactly right. They didn't want to cause their friends any more problems by giving them an anti-dote that, instead of making them better, made them worse.

'Okay, I think we should start by translating all the letters and numbers to what the chemicals that they represent,' Noah said to Esme as he lifted a pen and pad from the countertop. 'I'll do that, and you get the equipment we need to build this.'

Noah pointed at a diagram in the book. It was a drawing of glass jars and little glass pipes that all joined together to make one complicated structure.

Noah had read about the periodic table in a book his Nana had bought him. Every chemical in the world can be written down as a series of letters and numbers. In the instructions in the notebook, there were lists of these codes and when to add them to each other and whether to heat them or not.

He began to translate the letters into a long list of chemicals, looking

at a chart on the wall to make sure
he was getting them right.

H2O - Water
K - Potassium
Ge - Germanium

The list was 9 ingredients long.
Each had to be added in precise
amounts and in the exact order the
instructions said. Once he wrote
the list he turned on some digital
scales which Esme had found and
began to weigh out the exact
amount of each ingredient into little
glass bowls.

From across the countertop, Mrs
Graham was watching carefully as
the child scientists got to work. As
Esme put the final piece of the
equipment in place, a test-tube

underneath a little tap, Noah lifted
the first little bowl and raised it
above the beaker at the start of the
experiment.

At that moment, Mrs Graham
started banging on the side of the
tub and jumping up and down.
Noah, who was just about to
release the first ingredient stopped
and looked at the tiny woman. She
was shaking her head and shouting
something. Noah opened the lid of
the tub and very clearly heard a
very high pitch, 'noooooooo! Water
first!'

Noah looked back at the book and
realised that he had almost missed
the first step of the experiment.
Water. Thank goodness Mrs
Graham had been there, although

she did cause this whole mess to begin with so it was hard for Noah to be thankful.

Noah carefully measured out the right amount of water into a little glass beaker and the experiment began. He added the chemicals in order, stirring when it said he should, leaving it when it said he should. By the time either chemical had been added nothing had happened. The blue, yellow, red and white crystals sat in a little pile in the bottom of the water and slowly began to dissolve.

Noah lifted the ninth little bowl which, instead of crystals had a clear liquid in it. He gently poured the liquid in and just when he thought nothing was going to happen the mixture burst into life. It began to fizz and bubble and spit little drops all over the sides of the beaker.

Noah looked at the book. The next instruction was to quickly push the rest of the apparatus into the flask and allow the experiment to finish its course. Noah grabbed the flask and then the end of the rest of the equipment. The end was a rubber stopper with a narrow, curly glass tube which ran through the middle of it. He gently pushed the stopper into the top of the flask and stepped back from the counter.

Esme and Noah watched as the mixture fizzed. Firstly a white set of Bubbles set off up the curly tube and started to condense into a white liquid which whizzed along another pipe and into the dropper at the end. Suddenly the liquid in the beaker turned bright red and within a minute the dropper was filled with a pink coloured liquid. The final few minutes of the reaction sent a purple liquid shooting through the tubes and instantly turning the final result into what looked like a thick purple glue. As suddenly as the reaction had begun it was over.

'I hope we got it right, Esme,' Noah said, 'what does the book say we do now?'

Esme lifted the book and read out the final instruction.

'Use the dropper to fill a bottle with the anti-dote, one drop will cure any effects of the potions. Don't overuse it or you will double the cure and double the effect.

'That second bit feels important,' Noah said, 'we don't want to accidentally create any tiny heads or giants.'

He looked around the room and upon finding a little bottle, he transferred the sticky, purple liquid into it.

You won't get away with this!

Noah and Esme looked at their weird collection of things; an old toy box with three tiny people in them, a plastic tub with a tiny woman inside and a bottle of sticky, purple liquid. They'd achieved a lot in one afternoon but they had a problem. They had no idea what to do next.

'We're going to have to tell someone,' Esme eventually said, 'a grown-up will know what to do. Should I go get my mum?'

Noah didn't have any better ideas. He nodded and turned his gaze back to Mrs Graham in her plastic tub. Seeing a fully grown person shrink down to the size of a doll was a fascinating thing to see. You don't notice how amazing humans are until something makes you pay attention. Noah hadn't thought about it before, but human bodies are amazing and can do amazing things. He spent the time that Esme was away getting his Aunt watching Mrs Graham's every move.

'Oh no! What have you done?' Auntie Sue shouted as soon as she walked into the garage. She looked at Mrs Graham in disbelief. 'Why would you do something like this?

How did you do something like this?' she went on.

'Mum, listen. Noah worked out that Mrs Graham was trying to sabotage our football team. She's been disguising herself and lying to the school that she is called Ermentrude Glock. She is the one who caused all the weird things to happen to my teammates,' Esme was still very angry as she told the story. She was very competitive and cheating made her angriest of all.

She went on to explain how they had shrunk the Grahams down and got Mrs Graham to explain to them how to make the antidote. As she told the story she could see that her mum was now angry as well.

'You won't get away with this!' she shouted pointing her finger to the tiny Mrs Graham in the tub in the countertop. Esme was competitive but her mum was even more so, particularly when it came to someone trying to cheat against her daughter.

Auntie Sue, Noah and Esme decided that they would take the Graham's straight to the police station. It is one thing to know how to shrink someone and want to take revenge but if anything else went wrong they didn't want to get into any more trouble.

Auntie Sue went to get the car and Esme and Noah carried the Grahams and the little bottle of antidote to the driveway and then gently laid them in the boot.

'I think this is the weirdest day of my life, Esme,' he said, 'I can't quite believe this is real.'

'I know,' Esme replied, 'just as long as that horrible purple stuff works on the others we will be okay . That's what matters. Thanks for helping Noah. I know you don't like getting in trouble.'

'No, but I do love experiments and investigating so this was a lot of fun when I wasn't scared,' Noah replied as the car arrived outside the police station.

As they got out of the car, Auntie Sue bent over so that her face was close to the two children's faces.

'Now listen. Let me do the talking in here. I don't want you to say the wrong thing. We have to make sure that the police use that stuff you have made to save your friends. The championship depends on it. Okay? Let's go in.

The Police Station

Noah had never been inside a
police station. He had seen lots of
them in films and tv programmes
and he was excited to see all the
touch screen monitors and
futuristic gadgets that those TV
police stations had. When he
walked through the doors he was
instantly disappointed. This police
station looked nothing like the
stations he'd seen on TV. This
station had a very boring looking,
brown, wooden counter, a blue
notice board with posters that were
out of date and some blue plastic
chairs.

Behind the blue counter was a very tall man in a police uniform. He had grey hair and a big, bushy moustache. Noah noticed a badge on the man's chest, Constable A. Smyth. Constable A. Smyth seemed to not notice that Auntie Sue, Esme and Noah were even there, he was looking at his phone and, from the noises his phone was making, Noah could tell he was playing Shape Shift. Shape Shift was the game Noah's dad let him play on his phone when they had to wait somewhere for a long time and Noah got restless.

'Ahem,' Auntie Sue said loudly, 'Excuse me, sorry to interrupt but we need to report a crime.'

Constable Smyth jumped at the sound of Auntie Sue's voice and as he did he threw his phone into the air which dropped into a mug on the desk sending coffee splashing up into the poor man's face. Noah tried not to laugh as the brown liquid dripped off the ends of the officer's moustache.

'I'm sorry, I didn't hear you come in. Oh, no, my phone, ugh, one second please,' he spluttered drying his face with one hand as he shook coffee off his phone with the other. 'I do hope it's waterproof,' he continued.

Auntie Sue, ignoring most of what the man had just said, got straight down to business,

'Last week, I am sure you have heard, there were some very strange happenings at Oak Heath Primary. Several members of the school football team, the reigning champions, began to come down with some rather unique ailments. It had been unclear, until now, what exactly had caused these poor children to suffer shrinking, and swelling and other awful things. My clever daughter and her equally clever cousin have solved the mystery. I want to report the crime of poisoning and sabotage of a football team and name the Graham family as the culprits.'

Auntie Sue wasn't speaking in her normal voice. She sounded a bit like a newsreader or an MP for some reason and she was standing in a very strange way with her chin pointing up slightly as if she was very posh. Constable Smyth was writing furiously on a slightly wet note pad. He was struggling to keep up with Auntie Sue's speech. After 30 seconds of silence, he looked up and said,

'The Grahams. The Grahams that own Grahams Bubbles? Well, have you any evidence it was them? We can't just go and arrest such well-known people without any evidence.'

Before the Constable could finish speaking, Esme whipped open one of the boxes to reveal the tiny Graham family inside,

'Is this enough evidence?' she said looking at the officer, 'Mrs Graham will confess to you if you find a room that is quiet enough to hear her speak.'

Constable Smyth's mouth dropped open. He couldn't quite believe what he was seeing. He had heard about what had happened at the school but seeing tiny little people like this, in reality, was very different to imagining it.

'Well, I, um, well. I suppose if they confess then it won't be so hard to investigate. Bring that box of Grahams and follow me to room 7a, and we can talk more there,' he said and led the three down a corridor to a small room with a table in it and a big mirror on the wall, just like on TV.

Esme set the box down on the table and, along with Auntie Sue and Noah, watched Constable Smyth walk up and down the room scratching his head. It was obvious that he didn't know what to do. That is understandable, it must be the first time someone had come to report a crime and brought the villains along with them in a toy box.

'Constable Smyth,' Noah spoke for the first time since entering the station, 'We forgot to mention that we have the antidote, Esme and I made it from instructions that we found in the Graham family lab. I think I know what we need to do.'

Constable Smyth stopped pacing around the room and looked at Noah. He couldn't believe he was going to ask for advice from such a small boy but he was out of ideas and still in shock from the whole situation he had found himself in.

'Well, go on then kid,' he said, 'tell me what we should do.'

Noah, walked over and put his hands on the table, leaned forward over the open box and said, 'there are four small Grahams and there are seven members of the football team who we need to give anti-dote too. We don't want to risk giving the anti-dote to the football team, in case Esme and I made a mistake when we made it. We also

don't want to give it to all four
Grahams before we know that it
works because then they wouldn't
help us if we ran out. So, I suggest
that we choose one of the
Grahams and give them the anti-
dote to see if it works, and then if it
does, give it to the team and then
finally the remaining Grahams.
Once the four Grahams are normal
size again, you can charge them
with the crime of trying to cheat at
football.'

Noah stood up and folded his
arms. He knew it was a good plan
and he could tell from Constable
Smyth's face that he thought it was
a good plan too. He reached into
his pocket and pulled out the little
bottle on anti-dote and set it on the
table.

Constable Graham lifted it and as he swirled it around said, 'You're full of surprises, aren't you. Who would have thought such a small boy could have such a big idea. I think your plan is perfect. I will get another officer to come to help me and we can get to it right away. You will have to watch from in there though, 'he said pointing at the mirror.

Miri Graham takes the antidote

Noah, Esme and Auntie Sue were led into a tiny little room on the other side of the mirror. It was just like you've seen on TV, the mirror was a window on the other side and they could see everything that was happening next door. A policewoman came in and flicked a switch on the wall which turned on the microphones in the next room. The three sat quietly and listened, all they could hear was the high pitched talking of the Graham family in Esme's old toy box but they couldn't make out what they were saying.

After a few moments, Constable Smyth and another officer walked back into the room with a saucer, a water bottle and some gloves. The other officer reached into the toy box and lifted out Miri Graham, who let out a very high pitched but very quiet scream. I imagine that if you were very small being lifted into the air by a full-sized human would be like being flung around by a T-Rex and would be very frightening.

Meanwhile, Constable Smyth struggled to get the rubber gloves onto his big hands. The three perched in the next room could hear him making little grunts of frustration as he pulled and tugged at the rubber and tried to wiggle his fingers into the fingers of the gloves. Once he had finally managed to complete his simple task he poured a few tiny drops of the water onto the saucer and then added a single drop of the anti-dote into it.

'Now, little Miss Graham. On this saucer is the anti-dote to the mixture that made you small. If you drink it we hope that you will go back to normal size,' Constable Smyth was leaning over Miri and for some reason was shouting. I'm not sure why he felt that small people wouldn't be able to hear him as well. He also seemed not to notice that the louder he got the harder Miri was pressing her hands over her ears.

What happened next was astounding. Miri slowly walked over to the saucer, cupped her hands and drank some of the liquid. She winced a little, it clearly didn't taste very nice, but she continued to drink it until it was almost all gone. After a few minutes of silence, she started to jump around and looked very confused. She was patting her hands on her legs and arms and head but it didn't look like anything was happening.

All of sudden, there was a burst of movement, and Miri very quickly grew back to her normal size. Her legs and arms shot out from the spot where the small version of her had been standing and in an instant, there was a normal-sized child on the table. As her right leg had grown out quickly her foot had pushed the toy box with her family in it onto the floor. Everybody stared in amazement at what they had seen. The anti-dote had worked.

'I'm back to normal. Thank you, ' Miri said staring at her full-sized hands as if they were the first hands she had ever seen.

There was no time to stare though because the other three Grahams had escaped the toy box and were now running around the room trying to find a way out. Noah laughed as he watched the two police officers chase the tiny Grahams around the room. It was like watching a farmer chasing escaped chickens around a farmyard. Noah wished he'd had a phone to record a video of it.

Eventually the other Grahams were rounded up and out back into their toy box and Miri was given some crisps and a drink.

'Right then. We best go and give some of this to the football team,' Constable Smyth said looking at the mirror.

The School Nurse

Within an hour Noah, Esme, Auntie Sue and Constable Smyth were in the school nurse's office surrounded by the members of the football team with all of their strange appearances. In one corner was Maya Nowak who was lying on a sofa that she was almost bigger than. There was a group of players stood on a table who had been shrunk down to 30 cm tall and across the room was Samir who was lying on the floor with pillows propping up his huge head. It was possibly the weirdest sight that Noah had ever seen and after the day he had had that was saying something.

A few minutes passed and Nurse Suarez and Mr Fowler came into the room. Everyone at school joked that Mr Fowler was in love with Nurse Suarez so when they came in together there was a little giggle in the room. Mr Fowler did seem nervous but that could have just been because of what was about to happen.

'Okay, everyone,' Mr Fowler said looking around the room and the very strange collection of people around him, 'Helena, sorry I mean, Nurse Suarez, is going to give each of the afflicted members of the team a little drop of this antidote that Noah and Esme have created and hopefully, I mean, you will all DEFINITELY be back to normal soon. It has been, um, yes, tested and it seems to work. Samir, you can go first, that big head looks very painful.'

Nurse Suarez took her time and went around the room treating all her patients. Every time one of them grew to normal size, deflated, or had their head return to normal a gasp went up from everyone watching, followed by a round of applause. The noise in the room was the same as what you hear at a circus when the acrobats are throwing themselves through burning rings or off trapeze bars. There were no clowns though.

After about 25 minutes the room was full of normal-sized and normal-shaped children and their parents. Everyone was hugging and talking and laughing. One by one, people were coming up to Noah and Esme and thanking them and giving them hugs. Noah did not like when people he didn't know that well hugged him, and especially not if they'd been tiny for a few days and not had a bath.

As people were sharing stories of what it felt like to be a balloon or to have your feet swap sides Noah's Dad arrived with 6 pizzas.

'I am sure you are all starving,' he said, 'some of you have only eaten crumbs for the last few days.' He opened the boxes and then walked over to Noah and ruffled his hair and said,

'Well, Professor Curiosity, it seems that you haven't killed the cat after all. If anything, you've saved the day.'

'What cat, Dad?' Noah asked and for a reason he didn't understand, all the adults laughed.

'The day isn't saved yet,' Esme said, 'we still have to win on Saturday and we haven't been able to train all week.'

The Big Game

On the day of the final game of the
championship the local paper had
the headline, 'Justice for Oaky's?'
and a story that told the whole town
of the Graham family's plot to
sabotage the Oaky's football team.
It had pictures of the Grahams sat
angrily on a sofa in the police
station. The article went on to say
that, although they were guilty, they
weren't going to go to prison due to
an intervention by the Oaky's team
and their parents.

Instead of being put before the
courts for their crime, it had been
agreed between the Oaky's team,

the police and the Grahams that
their punishment would be as
follows;

- Miri and Jason would not be
  allowed to play in the final
  and instead would have to
  dress up as the team mascot
  for Oaky's which was a bright
  orange oak leaf.
- Mr and Mrs Graham were not
  allowed to watch the match
  but instead had to wait in the
  Oaky's changing room to
  clean the boots and smelly
  kits once the match was
  over.
- If Oaky's won, the Grahams
  would have to present the
  trophy to Esme as the
  winning captain.

If they did all three things, everyone agreed that no further punishment would be necessary. Handing over the trophy to Esme would be so humiliating for them that they'd regret messing with the Oaky's team for a very long time.

As Noah arrived at the ground, he saw his friend James. James went to Bunks, but like Noah, wasn't in the football team. James was really smart and Noah loved talking to him about space and science. Noah's Dad and James' mum went to the same gym, although Noah couldn't quite remember the last time his Dad had actually gone to the gym.

James and Noah decided to watch the game together. They didn't understand why people from different schools couldn't just be friends. To Noah, football was just a game, but don't tell Esme he felt that way. James and Noah watched as the teams came out. There was a big crowd around the pitch, perhaps the biggest crowd one of these matches had ever seen. The events of the past week had made this a must-see game.

'This game makes Esme the record holder for most games ever and if she scores she's the highest ever goalscorer too,' Noah said reading the stats from his notebook.

'Is there a stat about whose parents shout the loudest, Noah?' James asked after one parent shouted their encouragement so loudly that they started coughing halfway through their sentence.

The game kicked off and was instantly fiercely competitive. The crowd was so loud, that after five minutes, Noah had to put on his ear defenders. Parents were screaming phrases that didn't mean much to Noah, things like; 'Line it!' 'Man on' and the most confusing of all, 'square ball.'

Esme was playing one of the best games Noah had seen her play. She seemed to be all over the pitch, popping up at one end to defend Oaky's goal from attack and then seconds later hitting a shot at the Bunks keeper.

After 88 minutes it was still 0-0 but Oaky's were applying a lot of pressure. The team had come out at half-time and were playing as if someone had given them rocket fuel to drink. They were faster, tackling harder and passing with more accuracy than ever. Esme and Samir had both had shots hit the post and a Bunks player had accidentally passed the ball between his keeper's legs but a muddy puddle on the pitch stopped it from becoming an own goal. That was all about to change.

Esme gathered the ball to her feet just outside the Oaky's penalty box. She looked up at the Bunks goalkeeper and, as if someone hit a switch in her mind, she charged forward. Bunks players attempted

to tackle her but her feet seemed to
be moving at the speed of light.
They would reach their foot
towards the ball to take it from her
but by the time their foot reached
its destination the ball was gone,
and Esme moved off in another
direction. She put it through players
legs and twisted and turned so
much that other players fell over.

She was approaching the goal. It
was as if everything was slowing
down, as people expected to see a
wonder goal. She planted her left
foot beside the ball and bent her
right foot back to take a shot but
before she could take her shot one
of the Bunks Defenders threw
himself towards Esme, he was
trying to take her out. He had no

plan to take to the ball, he wanted to foul her.

He was moving fast, but Esme saw him coming and with a move that seemed to defy the laws of science, she flicked the ball towards him and hit him right on the nose before bouncing back and into the path of Samir who had run the whole way up the pitch after Esme. He collected the ball and flicked it over the top of the Bunks defender, who was now lying on his back holding his nose. The ball was going to reach Esme but would end up just behind her. Suddenly, she leapt forward and bent her legs behind her as if she was a diver leaping from a diving board. The whole crowd breathed in and every second seemed to last a minute. Then … boom, everything sped up suddenly as Esme struck the ball with her heel before falling to the ground and doing something that looked very like a backflip. The ball had hit the top corner of the net so hard that it was still there, caught in the netting.

The Bunks goalkeeper was lying in the puddle that had saved their blushes earlier. Esme had scored, the crowd erupted with cheers. Noah looked around and realised that it wasn't just Oaky's fans who were cheering. Everybody at the game was cheering. What they had seen was very special, Esme had beaten the whole Bunks team, almost on her own. She had scored a wonder goal. She was now the all-time leading scorer in the Primary School Championship history. She had also scored the winning goal, as the ref blew the whistle before Bunks could kick-off. Esme was a hero.

As promised, the Graham family walked out onto the pitch with the trophy to present it to the Oaky's team. Esme walked up and lifted the trophy high above her head as the crowd cheered. Noah was so proud of his cousin and his school. They had done it.

As he watched the celebrations he didn't realise that the team were chanting his name and that Esme was walking trophy towards him with the trophy.

'Come join the team celebration, Noah,' she said, 'we couldn't have done it without you, Professor Curiosity.'

Noah smiled and joined the team in their celebrations and later on at Pizza Fantastico with all of their families.

What a week it had been. Maybe, there was a fine when curiosity did kill the cat, but this time, Professor Curiosity won the cup.

Printed in Great Britain
by Amazon

53560656R00081